Moonlight
Tales

Illustrated by Alison Edgson

STRIPES PUBLISHING
An imprint of the Little Tiger Group
1 Coda Studios, 189 Munster Road, London SW6 6AW

A paperback original
First published in Great Britain in 2013

ISBN: 978-1-84715-392-0

A CIP catalogue record for this book is available from the British Library.

Printed and bound in the UK

2 4 6 8 10 9 7 5 3

Moonlight Tales

stripes

CONTENTS

THE YULETIDE LOG
Michelle Misra   p7

THE MAKING OF
THE MOON
Michael Broad   p25

MOLLIE
Penny Dolan   p45

HOME FOR CHRISTMAS
Liss Norton   p65

THE SQUIRREL AND
THE SNOWMAN
Caroline Juskus   p87

MAKING FRIENDS
Linda Chapman   p107

LITTLE STICK TAIL AND THE MOON DEVIL
Lucy Courtenay   p127

THE STORY KITTEN
Holly Webb   p147

THE MOON THIEVES
Elizabeth Baguley   p165

OBI'S UMBRELLA
Caroline Pitcher   p185

THE YULETIDE LOG

Michelle Misra

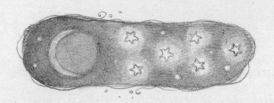

"It's snowing! Look!" Barney raised his paw and pointed through the window of the riverbank lodge. He slapped his paddle-shaped tail excitedly. "Oh, when will Papa get home?"

"Soon, Barney," Ma Beaver sighed. "He'll be back very soon." She looked out of the window and beyond the reeds. Her whiskers twitched and her small ears quivered. It was dark outside and little flurries of snow were racing across the night sky. The light of the moon flitted across the riverbank, making the water appear like a mirror.

It was some time ago that Pa Beaver and Gramps had set off to get the Yuletide log. If they weren't back soon, the entrance to the lodge would ice over and then they'd never be able to make their way in. The snow was falling heavily now with big blobby snowflakes settling on the pond.

"Come on, kits." Barney's mother dragged her children away from the window. "Time to put up the decorations. You make a start on the fireplace while I get the pudding out of the oven."

Barney turned to his little sister, Polly, with excitement. There was so much to do for the Winter Feast tomorrow night. He didn't know where to start. Their home wasn't big,

there were only two chambers – one for sleeping and one for dining – but they would certainly do their best to make it look festive! The delicious smells of Ma Beaver's baking wafted through the air as the two young beavers set to work. Winter nut pudding with maple and cherry bark. Yum!

Barney and Polly dragged a box out from under their bed, and began pulling out all sorts of decorations – red berries, mistletoe, glistening branches.

"I remember when I made this..." Polly held up a fir cone on a ribbon and placed it over the fireplace.

"And we have to put this up," cried Barney, gnawing through a long line of ivy and starting to hang it across the mud walls.

As the two young beavers worked hard to decorate the chambers, Ma Beaver came back in and placed her winter nut pudding on the table. It was topped with a piece of holly in the centre.

At that moment, there was a gust of wind, shaking the lodge and sending a chill through the chambers.

"Come on," Ma Beaver shuffled over to the young kits. "It's time for bed. Look," she pointed out of the window to where the sun was just starting to rise over the

surrounding hills.

"What about Pa and Gramps?" asked Barney.

"They'll be back before you know it," said Ma Beaver, glancing quickly at the sun before turning back to her young.

"Are we the only animals who sleep in the day?" Barney asked, letting out a loud yawn.

"Not the only ones," smiled Ma Beaver. "Now, hop into bed." She gave the kits a couple of wooden sticks to gnaw on and soon the baby beavers settled down. Their stockings were already hanging from little hooks on their bedposts.

"Tell us the story of Great-great Grandpa Beaver again," Barney said as he looked up at the portrait above their bed.

Ma Beaver smiled. "On a cold winter's

night," she began, "when the moon was high in the sky and there wasn't a noise in the house to wake a water rat..."

Barney snuggled down under his blanket as his mama carried on speaking. "Great-great Grandpa Beaver set off on his way..."

Barney's eyes started to close. Great-great Grandpa Beaver had been the oldest and bravest of beavers − the first of their kind to bring back the Yuletide log. It had become a beaver tradition for them to burn a part of that old log, along with the new, in the first fire of winter to protect them for the year ahead.

"It was dark when Great-great Grandpa started his journey," Ma Beaver went on, "but that didn't trouble him. He knew exactly where he had to go − over high

mountains and deep valleys – to get to the redwood forest."

"He was a long way from home, wasn't he, Mama?" Polly chipped in.

"He was indeed," Ma Beaver nodded. "But soon he reached the forest and gnawed a tree down with his bare teeth. The way back was tough, though. He had to roll the tree along the ground with his feet, until he reached water. Then he was able to swim with it, until he came to—"

"A waterfall!" Barney interrupted.

Ma Beaver smiled patiently.

"The tree tumbled down the waterfall, with Great-great Grandpa clinging on for dear life.

Finally he reached dry land, but then he had to do battle with a mink who tried to steal the tree from him. Great-great Grandpa nearly lost it, but he fought hard and won it back. The journey took him under many moons and across many crevasses. He even had to use the log like a beam, to get across a ragged ravine until finally, he reached home," Ma Beaver finished.

The lodge felt warm and snuggly and soon the two young kits were fast asleep with dreams of a brave warrior beaver in their heads...

Ma Beaver smiled. She looked out over the water's edge as the snow continued to fall. Just where were Papa and Gramps? She waddled down the tunnel to the water, but she didn't want to go too far and leave

her kits alone. As she stared out into the darkness, she felt a cold chill, like a stone, in the pit of her stomach.

When Barney woke, the lodge felt cold after the cosy warmth of bedtime. He shivered and stretched his legs. His sister was snoring softly. His mama was asleep in the rocking chair by the window. Papa and Gramps clearly weren't back yet.

Barney thought hard. He couldn't just sit there, waiting. He would go and look for them. After all, he was descended from the bravest and noblest of beavers.

Quick as a flash, he stole past Ma and hurried down the tunnel, his paddle flapping from side to side. The tunnel ducked down and left, and soon Barney hit water. It was even colder than the lodge and there was a strong current, which seemed wrong. Barney pushed himself forward, kicking out with his webbed feet until he reached the surface.

He sniffed the air, his head bobbing one way, then the other. Something wasn't right. He could feel it in his bones and in the pull of the water.

Quickly he swam upstream, his little feet propelling him onwards, his tail acting like a rudder. It was eerie outside and there might be many a wild predator who would be glad for a tasty young beaver like him.

Barney felt frightened as he scented the air. His sight wasn't good, but his sense of smell was strong and something felt wrong.

"Papa…" he cried, his teeth chattering. "Gramps…" His voice echoed out over the woods.

By the watery sunlight, Barney reached the end of the pond. He could see the criss-crossing branches and twigs that made up the dam, but there was rushing water plunging through it. So that was why there was a current in their pond! If the dam burst, their lodge would be swept away. Then Barney saw Pa and Gramps, trapped under a tree trunk against the dam!

"Papa!" Barney rushed forward. "What happened?"

"We were chopping down a tree for the Yuletide log, but it fell on top of us and smashed through the dam," his papa called urgently. "Can you push it off?"

Barney scampered up. He heaved and heaved, but he couldn't move the trunk. It was too heavy. He looked over his shoulder. There wasn't time to go back and get help.

"Use your teeth, Barney," Pa Beaver said.

One ... two ... three sharp bites — nothing. The log didn't move. Barney wasn't making any progress. But his teeth were sharp. He tried again, gnawing and gnawing, until a noise like a drill sounded throughout the forest. Wood chips flew.

Kerchung!

The tree split in two and Papa and Gramps slipped into the pond. More water was gushing through the hole in the dam now. There wasn't a moment to lose.

Quickly the beavers set to work, passing each other sticks and branches to plug the hole before finally packing it with mud. It was dangerous work and they could have been carried off at any point, but just when Barney thought that they were never going to manage it, the water stopped.

Pa Beaver gave his son a hug. "You've done it! You've done it, Barney!"

"It's getting late! We must get back to the lodge," said Gramps. "Can you give me and your pa a paw to help with the log?"

The three beavers grabbed one half of the log that Barney had split in two and swam, gently pushing it through the water until they reached the lodge entrance. They paddled up, tugging the log behind them.

Ma Beaver was the first to meet them. "Thank goodness you're back!" she cried. "I've lost Barney... He's missing!" Then she saw her little kit behind Pa Beaver and reached out her paws to hug him.

Quickly Pa Beaver told her everything – how the tree had fallen on them as they'd gnawed it down, damaging the dam, and how Barney had rescued them before helping to block up the hole together.

Ma Beaver was cross that Barney had gone off on his own, but she couldn't be angry for long – not when her family was safe and sound. She looked at her son. He really was a daring little beaver.

And now the light was just starting to fade. The day of the Winter Feast was almost upon them. Polly ran into the dining chamber excitedly.

"Here's the Yuletide log," said Pa Beaver, placing a piece of the new log in the grate, along with the old embers from last year. Then he bent down to light it and the flames licked over them. Barney danced round the fire.

Barney's heart skipped a beat — he could see the stockings by his bed, and they were spilling over!

"Mama! Papa!" he squeaked, pointing. "Can we open them?"

"Of course," Pa Beaver smiled, gathering his family in a big hug. "Let the Winter Feast begin!"

THE MAKING
OF THE MOON

Michael Broad

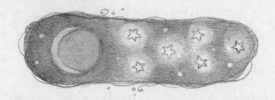

On the night of the annual Snow Festival, the owls of Winter Wood perched on the bare branches of the trees and looked towards the sky. The other woodland animals were gathered below – rabbits, badgers, hedgehogs and foxes, all waiting to celebrate the first snow of winter. The highlight of the festival was always the owls' amazing air show, led by the bird that spotted the first snowflake.

Orion the owl chick perched with his mama and sisters – Lyra and Vega. It was the chicks' first festival so they were all excited and each of them hoped they would be the first to spot the snowflake and lead this year's show.

"How do we know the snow is definitely coming tonight, Mama?" asked Orion, scanning the starry sky. The little owl loved to stargaze and was used to looking up.

"Because owls are the wisest of all the animals," replied Mama. "We know lots of things that other creatures do not and try to share our wisdom whenever we can."

"Orion's not wise," chuckled Lyra. "He's such a dreamer."

"I'm not a dreamer!" protested Orion.

"He's always stargazing in class," added Vega.

"Sometimes stargazers can be the wisest owls of all," said Mama, looking up at the Moon and smiling thoughtfully. "And I believe tonight is the perfect night to tell you all the legend of the Snow Festival and how the Moon came to be."

"*Wow!*" gasped the chicks, huddling together as their mother began the story.

☆

A long time ago, before the Moon was made, there was just the Sun in the sky. Only daytime animals could see the world and enjoy its beauty. The daylight was too bright for nocturnal animals and the night was too dark to see anything at all, so they kept bumping into each other and were very unhappy.

The only animals that could see in the dark were the owls, because their eyes were large enough to see by the distant starlight, and they spent every night guiding their nocturnal neighbours and describing their surroundings to them. Owls know lots of good words, but even they could not do justice to the natural beauty of the world, so the clever birds decided to put their minds together and find a way to light the night for everyone.

Owls gathered from miles around to discuss the problem and explore different

options, all except for one little owl named Luna. He spent so much time gazing at the stars that the other owls ignored him, believing that he was a dreamer and not at all wise like them.

☆

"Really?" gasped Orion, nudging his sisters.

"No way!" Lyra and Vega frowned, thinking that their mama had added bits to the story to make Orion feel better about being a dreamer and a stargazer.

"That's how the legend goes," smiled Mama. "It's how your grandmother told it to me and how my grandmother told it to her," she added, and continued with the story...

☆

The greatest minds worked for many weeks

and months. News of their challenge spread far and wide until every owl in the world flocked to Winter Wood to present their ideas. There were barn owls and eagle owls, tawny owls and snowy owls, all with their own wild and wonderful theories.

The owls tried filling the wood with night-blooming flowers to attract swarms of glowing fireflies, but the bugs were not bright enough to light up the night. They built wooden rods on the highest hills to draw electricity from storm clouds, but when the lightning struck, the wood turned to ash. They even tried filling the sky with flaming lanterns, but after a brief amber glow, the lights either went out or simply drifted away.

Every theory was considered and many were tried and tested, but each one failed to light the night for more than a few moments. The owls were about to admit defeat and break the sad news to the nocturnal animals when Luna hurried to the gathering.

"You haven't heard from me yet!" he said excitedly.

"How can you hope to succeed where the greatest minds have failed?" asked the great horned owl, who was the oldest and wisest owl and had overseen the trials. "All you have done is stare at the stars."

"It's true, I have been stargazing," said Luna. "But that's how I worked it out."

"Worked out what?" enquired the old owl.

"I was trying to work out where the Sun goes at night," explained Luna, using his wing to draw an imaginary arc above his head. "And watching the star patterns across the sky made me realize that the Sun doesn't really go anywhere at all."

"What a thing to say!" cried the great horned owl, flicking his tail feathers amid a roar of hoots and chuckles. "If the Sun doesn't move, then why is the night so dark?"

"I think the Sun stays in one place, like the stars, and it's the Earth that turns round. We face the Sun in the daytime," explained Luna, slowly turning his head to illustrate

his theory, "and it becomes dark at night because we're facing the other way."

This caused another riot of hoots and laughter from the assembled birds, but the great horned owl looked thoughtful and flapped his wings for them to quieten down.

"Wild theories are all very well," he said to Luna, "and yours is wilder than most. But they are no good unless you can test them. Even if you could prove this to be true, what good would it do us?"

"I don't know yet," Luna frowned.

"If the Earth is indeed moving, we cannot make it stop," the great horned owl added kindly. "And even if we could, half of the Earth would be without the Sun forever."

☆

"Luna's idea was silly," said Lyra. "I think he was just a dreamer."

"Like all stargazers," giggled Vega, tickling her brother, who had been staring at the sky.

"Stop it," protested Orion. "I'm looking for the first snowflake."

"Please don't tease your brother," said Mama as Lyra and Vega gave up watching the sky and began tickling each other. "And we won't know if Luna's idea was silly until the end of the story…"

The owls ignored Luna's theory, but he would not be disheartened. He thought about what the great horned owl had said, and looked to the stars again in search of an answer. If the Sun was still in the sky and

half of the Earth was facing the other way, there had to be a way to shine a little of its light on the dark side.

On the night the visiting owls were due to return home, a terrible snowstorm fell upon the land covering all of the woodland animals in a thick white blanket. The owls were safe up in the treetops so they swiftly set about saving the creatures on the ground, sweeping the snow away with their wings and packing it together in a large ball that they rolled for miles over hills and valleys.

Luna joined in, too, and as the snowball grew bigger and bigger, he watched it sparkle and glow in the dark, its white surface reflecting the distant starlight.

The little owl quickly scratched three

circles in the snow. One was the Earth and another was the Sun, and the last was the giant ball of snow. Luna looked at his circles and then up at the sky, realizing that if the snowball could be carried high enough, it would reflect the light from the hidden Sun! Certain that his plan would work, he flew off in search of the great horned owl to present his new idea.

The owls hooted and chuckled once again. But the old owl was wise enough to see that the little stargazer might be *wiser* than all of them, and that it would be foolish to dismiss his idea. So the great horned owl stepped forward and asked the world's owls to help carry out Luna's bold plan.

The birds all gripped the giant ball of snow with their sharp talons, flapped

their strong wings and eventually took flight, following Luna up into the night sky. Tiring under the enormous weight, the little stargazer urged them to follow him far above the clouds, until they could no longer see the ground below. Finally the owls released the snowball on the edge of space, where the air was icy thin. They hurled it even further until it slowed to a stop and lit up with a sudden brilliance, reflecting sunlight from the other side of the Earth!

A beautiful silver light shone down upon Winter Wood for the very first time and the animals all came out of their homes to see it. They blinked at the shining ball in the sky and cheered the returning owls with Luna up front.

From that night on, whenever the Sun set, the giant snowball was shining down. It came to be known as the Moon – though the woodland animals often call it Luna, after the clever little stargazer. And every year at the first snow of winter, they honour the owls with a Snow Festival and the owls put on an air show to celebrate the making of the Moon.

Just as the story finished, Orion saw a fluffy white snowflake drift down from the sky.

His sisters were busy playing and none of the other owls noticed it, so he looked to his mama and flapped his wings excitedly.

"There!" he gasped, pointing a wing skywards. "The first snowflake!"

The animals of Winter Wood cheered Orion as the year's first snowflake spotter. The snowflake was followed by another and another. Soon the sky was filled with snow and it covered the woodland in a crisp white blanket, signalling the start of the Snow Festival.

The owls made snowballs and hung them on the trees like bright, sparkling baubles, as the other woodland creatures began the celebrations. They made snow-owl sculptures and slippery slides, sang songs of snowflakes and danced in the powdery drifts. Meanwhile the owls prepared to re-enact the making of the Moon, and Mama showed Orion what to do.

The owls all took to the air and flew above the watching woodland animals. Orion was right up front and Mama was close behind with Lyra and Vega on either side. His sisters had to admit their brother was quite clever when he led the owls in the amazing air show.

Amidst the happy cheers and whistles from the ground, Orion swooped down to the trees and the other owls followed, grabbing the shining decorations in their talons. He soared back into the sky, flying higher and higher, and then the owls all launched their snowballs at the distant Moon, to ensure its light stayed bright for another year and to celebrate its creator, the little owl named Luna.

MOLLIE

Penny Dolan

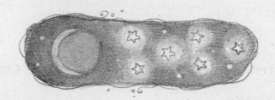

Outside, the fields were white in the moonlight. Inside the warm cottage, everyone was in bed. Only the two dogs lying beside the glowing fire were still awake.

"Go to sleep, Benjie," said the mother dog.

"I can't." The puppy shivered. "That noise frightens me."

"What noise?" she asked gently.

Suddenly, something howled down the chimney, like the wildest of wild things.

"That!" whimpered the puppy, snuggling tighter to his mother's side.

"That? It's only the wind. Don't be scared. Listen. I'll tell you a story. Once, years ago…"

The puppy put his head on his paws, ready to listen.

☆

One winter, this cottage was full of visitors. Some were busy making food. Others carried boxes and parcels in from their cars. There was even a sparkling tree that the children – Harry and his cousin Lucy – had decorated the night before.

A young dog, Mollie, was here, too. She was hardly older than a puppy and she wanted to join in with everything. She bounced about, barking in her

Off they went, all three, along the lane. They turned down a footpath that led across the fields. The afternoon sun shone, but frost still lay under the hedges and the ground was hard as ice under Mollie's paws.

Harry checked there were no sheep nearby before unclipping the dog's lead. "Off you go, silly girl!"

Mollie circled round, yelping her thanks. Then she trotted alongside them, sniffing the air eagerly.

After a while, they reached a stile. "What's that ridge up there?" asked Lucy, pointing. "Halfway up that hill?"

"That's the old road," said Harry. "Mum says the Romans used to walk along it."

Lucy's eyes lit up. "Oh, I love the Romans. We learned all about them in history and I've seen loads of programmes about them on TV. Please can we go up there?"

Harry frowned. "Actually, it's quite a long way."

"But we can walk really quickly, can't we?" begged Lucy. "Let's go! It's not fair if you've been there and I haven't."

"We'll walk a bit of the way," said Harry. That was what his mum always said. "Come on, Mollie!"

A twisty path led them through a small wood where Mollie snuffled about, startling the red-eyed pheasants.

"They're sillier than she is," laughed Harry.

Mollie barked joyfully. She didn't care.

By the time they left the wood, the sun had slid behind a small cloud. Lucy pulled her scarf tighter round her neck and Harry tugged on his red gloves.

"Maybe we should turn back now," said Harry.

"No way," said Lucy, marching fiercely onwards. "That ridge looks really close."

"It's still quite a long way," Harry told her. "Dad and I went up there last summer."

"You go back then if you want to," Lucy answered, stomping uphill. "Come on,

Mollie, you silly dog!"

Harry had to follow.

They reached the Roman road at last. By now the wind was stronger, ruffling up Mollie's fur. All the pup saw was a straight grassy path, but Lucy found it really interesting.

"Imagine, Harry! Maybe these stones are bits of broken Roman road." She bent down, searching the ground.

Mollie huffed and lay down. Harry waited, too, shivering. Then he glanced up and saw huge dark clouds sweeping across the sky towards them.

"Come on, Lucy! We've got to get home. That's snow coming." Even Mollie could hear how worried Harry was. "We'll go back the way Dad showed me

last summer. It's steep, but it'll be a lot quicker."

By now, the wind was much fiercer and carried the first snowflakes.

☆

"Mum, I don't like the wind in the story," worried the small puppy. "Will the silly dog be all right?"

"She'll be fine," said his mother firmly. "Her fur kept her warm and she wasn't tired at all. Just as well, seeing as what happened next..."

☆

"Here's the path," said Harry grimly when they reached a big rock. "We just follow the stream down the hill."

But the stream wasn't there any more. There was just a thin trickle of water dripping down over the icicles into the narrow gully below.

"I'll go first." Harry tried to sound confident. The path seemed much steeper than it did when he had been here last summer.

Harry edged his way down the first rocks. Lucy came next, slowly and nervously. Mollie stood at the top, paws slithering on the icy stones, waiting to follow them down.

Suddenly, as Harry turned sideways to check his footing below, his foot slipped from under him. He went tumbling down.

"Ow!" He fell heavily, with one leg twisted awkwardly.

"Harry!" screeched Lucy, quickly beside him. "Are you all right?"

Harry lifted his head, groggy after

his fall. "Think so." But then his face screwed up with pain. "No. I've hurt my stupid leg." He took off his glove and reached into his pocket. "Here's the phone," he said. "Call Dad, will you?"

Lucy stared in horror. "There's no signal," she gasped, "and I don't know the way home." Oh, how could she have been so stubborn? Besides, she couldn't leave Harry alone in the snow. "What can we do?" Lucy said, tearfully.

Mollie was watching Harry anxiously.

"You'll go, won't you girl?" he said. "Go home, Mollie. Get help."

The dog wagged her tail. Then she turned into the wind and all the scents and smells it brought.

"Can she find the way?" worried Lucy.

"Let's hope so," Harry said.

Mollie sniffed the wind, searching for the right direction. No, that way held the stink of motorway traffic. Not over that way. There was the distant smell telling her of a flock of huddled sheep. Then she turned her head slowly and there it was. The scent of home!

Mollie gazed at Harry and scraped the ground with her paw.

"Daft dog. What does she want now?"

he groaned.

Mollie swiftly snatched up the red glove lying next to him. Harry grabbed just as fast.

"Give it back. I need my glove," he shouted, but Mollie held on, growling softly. "I'm not playing tug-of-war, you silly thing," he said angrily.

"You clever girl," Lucy said, patting the dog's head. "Harry, she's not playing. She wants to take your glove with her."

"Oh!" Harry let his glove go. "Hurry, Moll. Please."

The young dog didn't look back. Glove between her teeth, she made her way through the icy gully and away among the trees below.

Where now? Where now? Within the wood it was harder to hold on to the right scent, but Mollie did not give up. She would not be a silly dog this time. She had to let everyone at home know about the children.

On she went and on – and then the fur on her back rose. She smelled danger – a thick peppery scent filling the air, blocking the trail. What could it be?

Then Mollie saw her enemy. An enormous fox, skulking in the shadows, eyes glittering and ears pricked up. She dropped the glove and growled as fiercely as she could. *Get out of my way! I have sharp teeth, too!*

Slowly, the fox lowered its head and slunk away, wary of a fight.

Mollie shook her head, trying to clear the foxy stink from her nose. Where had the trail gone now? *Come and help, you old wind!*

All at once, a flurry of snow swept through the trees. There it was: the scent of home, and faint voices calling.

Mollie seized the red glove and ran, fast, fast, fast. No time to lose. She raced across the darkened fields, scrambled over stone walls and pushed through the barred gates. Snowflakes swirled before her eyes and the cold air stung her nose, but Mollie raced on and on, letting the wind tell her the way.

Ahead were lights and torches. Ahead were grown-ups, calling out in worried voices, already searching for the missing children.

"Woof!" Mollie barked. She raced towards Harry's mother and dropped the red glove at her feet. "Woof!"

In moments, Mollie was surrounded.

"Harry's glove! Something awful has happened!" Mum said. "How are we going to find them?"

"Mollie will show us," said Dad as calmly as he could. "Where are they, Mollie? Take us, you good girl. Take us!"

It all ended well. Dad and Uncle Ben and the rest of the rescue party did reach Harry and Lucy. The children were brought home. They were shivering and shocked, but soon

they were warm again. Harry had to go to
hospital, but he was home again the next
day with his leg in plaster.

After that, everyone settled down for a
very happy holiday. The decorations on the
tree sparkled brightly and — although she was
not always perfectly behaved — nobody called
Mollie a daft dog or a silly girl any more.

Instead, they patted and praised her.
"Good dog," everyone said. "Clever Mollie."

☆

"So that silly young dog became a very
good dog indeed, Benjie. Whenever the
wind blows, she breathes in all the scents
the wind carries and listens to all the tales
it tells and it never makes her afraid."

The little puppy opened one eye. "Mum,
I liked that story."

"Good. And you won't worry about the wind any more?"

"No, Mum."

They dozed on beside the flickering fire.

"Mum?" murmured the pup. "Isn't your name Mollie?"

"It is," said the mother dog, snuggling her pup closer. "Now go to sleep."

HOME FOR
CHRISTMAS

Liss Norton

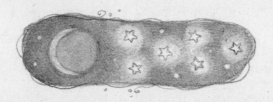

"Three days to Christmas!" sang Maddie McSqueak, a little wood mouse. She and her family were hurrying to the hazel grove to gather nuts for their Christmas feast. Maddie was the eldest, next came Arabella, then the twins Dommy and Theo and finally, baby Barnaby.

"Father Christmouse is gonna fill my stocking first!" cried Dommy.

"No, mine!" Theo insisted, pushing past him.

"No fighting, boys," Papa warned, as they pulled each other's whiskers.

"Barnaby doesn't fight," said Arabella, stroking her baby brother's downy ears. He was riding in their nut-collecting cart.

"Good Barney," Barnaby cooed.

They reached Fishbow Stream. The hazel grove was on the other side. Usually the stream was just a tiny trickle, shallow enough to paddle through, but today it was a rushing torrent.

"How will we get across?" said Mama, climbing down the bank for a closer look.

"Careful, Mama," Maddie warned.

Suddenly, Mama slipped. "Eek!" she squeaked. She scrabbled desperately at the bank, trying to get a foothold, then plunged into the racing water.

"Millie!" yelled Papa. Letting go of the cart, he threw himself into the stream. "I'm coming!" he called. The cart began to roll down the bank, taking Barnaby with it. Maddie grabbed the handle. "Quick!" she cried, her heart thumping as she struggled to hold it.

Arabella and the twins ran to help, but the cart was too heavy. "Aah!" wailed Theo as the handle slipped through their paws and the cart went bouncing down the slope. Maddie snatched Barnaby clear just in time and they watched, horrified, as the cart careered into a boulder and tipped over.

"It's broke!" gasped Dommy.

"At least Barnaby isn't," Arabella said, squeezing his tiny paw.

"I want Mama and Papa," quavered Theo.

They all looked down at the stream. It was still roaring along, frothing around sticks and stones that tried to block its path. But there was no sign of their parents.

"Are they drownded?" Dommy sobbed.

"No, they'll be fine," said Maddie. She handed Barnaby to Arabella, then hugged the twins, hoping they couldn't tell how frightened she was.

"They'll be wet," Arabella said.

"They'll soon dry off at home by the fire," Maddie replied, trying to sound cheerful.

"Now, let's search along the bank for them. They can't have gone far."

"Time to go home," Maddie said much later, when it began to get dark. The little mice had searched all along the stream, but their parents were nowhere to be found.

"But what about...?" began Dommy.

"Mama and Papa will come home soon," Maddie said. She took one last worried glance at the rushing stream, then picked up Barnaby. They trooped home, a sad little procession with drooping heads and heavy hearts.

Indoors, Maddie reheated some leftover stew while Arabella laid the table, but nobody felt hungry. They kept running to the window in the hope of seeing Mama and Papa.

"Bedtime," said Maddie when they'd cleared away. Everyone went upstairs sadly, brushed their teeth and climbed into bed.

"I can't sleep without Mama and Papa," Arabella squeaked tearfully.

"No," agreed the twins in small voices.

"I'll tell you a story about their adventures," said Maddie.

They snuggled down in their beds, ready to listen, and Maddie tucked Barnaby into his walnut-shell cradle.

"Fishbow Stream carried Mama and Papa a long way," she began. "When the water slowed they swam to the bank and found themselves in a beautiful garden full of carnations, roses, bluebells and snapdragons."

"Flowers don't grow in winter," said Arabella.

"It was a magic garden," Maddie explained. "Mama and Papa picked some beautiful pink carnations to bring home. But when they tried to get out of the garden, they couldn't climb over the high walls or cross the stream."

"Are they stuck?" gulped Theo.

"No," Maddie said, stroking his head. "Clever Papa plaited a rope out of grass, tied a loop in the end and threw it high until it caught on a branch hanging over the wall. Then he and Mama climbed out of the garden, still holding tight to their flowers. And that's the first part of their 'Home for Christmas' adventure." Maddie gave them all a kiss. "Go to sleep now."

"What was on the other side of the wall?" asked Arabella.

"The woods," Maddie replied.

"Our woods?"

"Yes." Maddie pulled Barnaby's blanket up to his chin. He was already asleep. Theo and Dommy were struggling to keep their eyes open and Arabella was yawning. Maddie blew out the candle and climbed into bed.

Mama and Papa didn't come home that night, nor the next day.

The children prepared for Christmas, though nobody was looking forward to it any more. Arabella and Theo made hazelnut cookies and plum pudding, while Maddie and Dommy brought in wood for the fire and stacked it in the corner.

"Are they coming yet?" Arabella asked, every few minutes.

Dommy peeked out of the door to check, but the answer was always "No".

When it started to snow in the late afternoon, the children stared miserably out of the window at the dancing flakes. "Don't like snow today," sighed Theo.

Everyone knew what he meant – snowballing would be no fun without

Mama and Papa.

"Let's hear some more of the story, Maddie," said Arabella after tea. She led the twins over to the fire and they all sat round, gazing into the flames. Barnaby snuggled into Maddie's lap.

"Mama and Papa set off for home through the woods," Maddie began. "They found a holly bush full of scarlet berries and nibbled some as they walked. Soon it began to snow."

"Like here," said Dommy.

"Yes," agreed Maddie. "The snow made it hard to get along. Drifts built up on the path and snowflakes got in their eyes so they couldn't see where they were going. Then Mama spotted a door hidden under a tree root. She knocked and a mole opened the door and invited them in. You should have seen his waistcoat. It was really colourful! He had a bright smile, too, so Mama knew he'd help. She told him they were heading for Woodhanger Hill."

"That's near our house," Arabella said.

"One of the mole's tunnels led to the top of Woodhanger Hill," Maddie said. "He fetched lanterns and some nuts for a snack, then he took Mama and Papa to the start of a dusty tunnel."

"Was it dark in there?" asked Theo.

"Not with the lanterns," Maddie said.

"Mama and Papa aren't scared of the dark, anyhow," said Arabella.

"Mama and Papa hurried along the tunnel, but after a while it forked and they didn't know which way to go," continued Maddie. "'We have to go uphill,' said Mama, dropping a nut on the floor to see which way it rolled. It rolled to the right, so that way was downhill. Mama and Papa took the left tunnel and soon they came out on the top of Woodhanger Hill."

"What about Fishbow Stream?" asked Arabella. "Didn't they have to cross it to get to Woodhanger Hill?"

Maddie thought quickly. She'd forgotten about the stream. "The tunnel went under

the stream," she said. "So Mama and Papa got across without even knowing it."

"Are they on top of the hill now?" asked Dommy hopefully.

"Yes," said Maddie.

They all went to the window and looked out. It was very snowy and the hill was invisible in the darkness. "How will they get through the snowdrifts?" asked Arabella, tugging anxiously at one whisker.

"They got out of the flower garden," said Theo.

"And worked out which tunnel to take," Dommy added. "Getting down the hill is easy-peasy!"

As they went up to bed, Maddie wondered where Mama and Papa really were. The stream could have taken them miles.

She shivered. Perhaps it had carried them so far that they'd never come home again…

Next day was Christmas Eve and the children worked hard to decorate the house. They strung berries together to make Christmas garlands and looped them from the ceiling. Even Barnaby helped by picking up the berries they dropped. Then they dug up a little fir tree, brought it indoors and covered it with dried flowers.

That evening they hung their stockings by the fireplace. On Christmas Eve, Father Christmouse would visit every woodland home in his magical sleigh pulled by six glittering moths. He would fill all the stockings with tiny presents.

"Here's Father Christmouse's cookie," Arabella said, setting it on the windowsill.

Dommy and Theo poured honey into a bowl for the moths.

They all looked at each other miserably. Without Mama and Papa it didn't feel like Christmas Eve at all.

"It was still snowing when Mama and Papa came out of the mole's tunnel," said Maddie, when everyone was in bed. "They saw a light shining through the driving snowflakes and found a little crooked house. The shrew who lived there lent them her sledge – a beautiful red sledge with silver swirls."

"Mama loves pretty things!" cried Arabella.

"Did Mama and Papa ride on the sledge?" Theo asked eagerly.

"Yes," said Maddie. "They're whizzing down the hill right now."

"So they're almost home?" Arabella said, relieved.

"When we wake up tomorrow, they'll be here." Maddie gave them all a goodnight kiss. The wind whistled shrilly as she climbed into bed and she sighed. Surely Mama and Papa would never make it home in weather like this.

When Maddie woke, the bedroom smelled of flowers. Opening her eyes in astonishment, she saw a vase of pink carnations on top of the cupboard. Then the bedroom door opened and Mama and Papa hurried in. "Happy Christmas, sleepy-heads," they cried.

The children sprang out of bed. "You're home!" gasped Arabella, hugging them tightly.

Theo and Dommy charged around the room, leaping on and off beds and whooping.

"Ma-ma! Pa-pa!" shrieked Barnaby, shaking his poppy-seed rattle.

"When did you get back?" Maddie asked, overjoyed to see them.

"Last night. We've had quite an adventure," said Papa.

"A magic garden and grass rope adventure?" asked Arabella.

"Yes," Mama replied, surprised.

"With a tunnel?" Dommy asked. "And a waistcoaty-mole?"

"And a crooked house and a whizzy sledge ride?" added Theo.

Mama and Papa looked astonished. "How did you know?" said Papa.

"Maddie told us," Arabella said.

Mama and Papa gazed at Maddie. "You told stories," Mama gasped, "and we lived them! How did it happen?"

Maddie shook her head, bewildered.

She couldn't explain it. She'd made up
stories about Mama and Papa to stop
Arabella and the boys getting too upset.
She'd never guessed that they might come
true … but she was very glad they had.

"I don't know how it happened," she said,
beaming at her parents, "but my stories
have brought you home for Christmas. And
that's the most important thing." She threw
her arms round them. This was going to be
the best Christmas ever!

THE SQUIRREL
AND THE
SNOWMAN

Caroline Juskus

Once upon a time in a land far, far away there lived a little red squirrel called Firetail. She shared a drey with her brother, Conker, and their mother in the hollow of an old oak tree on the edge of a farm. Mother told them the tree had grown from a magical acorn providing the most delicious nuts to eat.

But this year's winter had lasted so long that the squirrels had eaten all their acorn stores and were surviving on scraps put out for the chickens. Then it snowed and snowed and the farmyard turned as white as the moon. The farmer shut the chickens and their food inside the henhouse and the family of squirrels grew very hungry.

"I'm so weak I can barely lift my tail," said Mother Squirrel.

"And I'm so cold and hungry my legs won't work," mumbled Conker.

Firetail felt cold and hungry, too, but she did her best to sound chirpy. "Don't worry," she said brightly, "I'll find us something good to eat." She scurried down the tree, hoping the farmer might have spilled something from the chickens' food bucket.

Her luck was in! A curling piece of potato peel sat in the snow. She clutched it in her paws and continued her search

behind the henhouse. As she did the sun came out and there, sparkling in the light, was a shimmering snowman! Firetail smiled at him, but the snowman gazed at her sadly. He had no mouth.

Firetail scrambled up his round belly. "Here," she said kindly, "I think you need this more than I do." She made him a mouth with her potato peel and the snowman smiled immediately!

"Thank you!" he cried. "How kind of you to help me. I'm Prince Filbert. Who are you?"

Firetail hadn't expected the snowman to speak! "You're a prince?" she exclaimed. "My name's Firetail."

"*Fire*tail!" the snowman gasped. "Then you'd better hop down in case you melt me!"

"Oh, my tail's not actually on fire," explained Firetail, but she hopped off all the same and sat on it to reassure him. "Are you a real prince?" she enquired.

"I was," said the snowman glumly, "until a wicked witch put a spell on me."

"A wicked witch?" Firetail was scared of witches. Conker had told her stories about them.

"I didn't know she was a witch," sighed the snowman. "She pretended to be a hungry

old lady so I made her a bowl of porridge and offered to take her home on my horse. We'd only gone a short distance when she cackled horribly and threw off her hood revealing a gruesome face and long wild hair. Then she conjured up a snowstorm and within moments I was swept away. I flew through the night in a flurry of snowflakes. When I found myself here this morning I discovered I was made out of snow!"

"Oh no!" exclaimed Firetail. "Then I must try to help you!"

"But you already have," said the snowman. "When I didn't have a mouth I couldn't tell anyone what the witch had done, and your kindness has sorted that. Now I just need to reverse the witch's spell before I melt in the sunshine and vanish forever.

The only trouble is, I don't know how, and the king and queen can't help me because they don't know where I am."

"Oh dear," worried Firetail. "Perhaps I could push you into the shade of the fir tree so you don't melt?"

"I think you're too small to move me," said the snowman miserably.

"Then I know," said Firetail. "I'll fetch a broken branch from the fir tree and hold it over your head!" And she did just that. All day she sat on the snowman's head and sheltered him until the sun set. Then tired and sleepy, she wished him goodnight.

"Thank you," said the snowman. "You've been very kind."

Firetail smiled and scurried back home.

"Where've you been?" asked Conker

when she came in. "More importantly, did you find any food?"

Firetail told him she'd found some potato peel, but had given it to a snowman. "He said he was a prince!" she chirruped.

"What a silly squirrel you are," grumbled Conker. "Snowmen can't talk!"

"This one could!" protested Firetail and they began to squabble.

Mother huddled them beneath her tail and soothed them with her story of the magic acorn that grew into their tree.

"Are all acorns magical?" asked Firetail. "Only I planted one by the barn and it hasn't turned into a tree or anything."

"Maybe you just have to be patient," said Mother, "though some acorns are less magical than others."

"Then let's dig it up and eat it," suggested Conker.

"But what if it *is* magic?" protested Firetail. "If it grows into an oak tree we'll have lots more acorns in the years to come."

"I'm starving *now*," grumbled Conker.

Mother reassured him. "By morning the snow may have melted," she said, "and with the chickens back in the yard we'll have lots of juicy scraps."

Conker hoped she was right, but Firetail was worried. If the snow melted, then so would Prince Filbert!

Luckily for the snowman, next morning the snow was thicker than ever. Conker and Mother were most disappointed.

"Don't worry!" cried Firetail. "I'm sure I can find us something to eat."

"Don't feed it to the snowman," grumbled Conker, who was still too weak to go with her.

"I won't," said Firetail, who had quite another plan! If her acorn was magic it might be able to reverse the witch's spell. Instead of turning into an oak tree it might turn the snowman back into a prince!

She headed to the barn and began to dig for the acorn, but after a few minutes all she'd uncovered was the corner of a rat trap. There were lots around the farm, baited with cheese. Sometimes Mother flipped them over and when they sprang shut she removed the bait. Firetail wondered if she could do the same. If she had cheese for Conker she could use the acorn to help Prince Filbert.

But the rest of the trap was buried deep in the snow and Firetail was frightened she might trap her paws. To make matters worse, it was snowing heavily and no sooner did she scrape away a snowflake than another quickly settled in its place. It was the end of the day before she uncovered the trap. With a brave sweep of her tail she flipped it over and the trap snapped shut. Exhausted and cold, Firetail carefully teased out the cheese. With food for Conker and the trap out of the way, she unearthed the acorn and ran to find the snowman before it grew dark.

"Prince Filbert," Firetail called brightly. "I've got something that might help you!" She showed him her acorn and explained that some acorns could work magic. "You're so kind," said the snowman, "but don't you want to eat it? You told me your family was very hungry."

"We can eat this!" chirruped Firetail, waving the cheese.

She placed the acorn where the snowman's heart should be and he told her all about his palace that stood in the Faraway Wood surrounded by oak trees.

"If I do turn back into a prince," he said, "I'll take you and your family there and you'll always have lots of nuts to eat."

"Oh, thank you!" said Firetail. Hoping her acorn would work some magic, she ran home to give Conker the cheese.

Her little brother was overjoyed and shared it with Firetail and Mother. Firetail told them about the Faraway Wood full of acorns.

"You don't still believe the snowman's a prince, do you?" Conker yawned.

"Of course I do," said Firetail.

Mother squirrel wrapped them in her tail and, with food in their bellies, they fell fast asleep.

When they awoke the next morning, the snow had melted.

"Oh no!" cried Firetail. "What if Prince

Filbert has melted, too?" She leaped from the tree and ran to find him, but when she got there all that remained were two lumps of coal, a curl of potato peel and her acorn floating in a warm puddle.

Her acorn hadn't been magic at all.

"Poor Prince Filbert!" she sobbed. "I'm so sorry I couldn't help you and now it's too late. You've melted away and I'll never get to see you again." With tears in her eyes she scurried home.

"I told you he wasn't a prince," said Conker. "Now let's find some of the chickens' scraps!"

"Just a moment," said Mother. "Listen!"

Firetail and Conker pricked up their ears.

"Firetail? Firetail!" Someone was calling her.

"It's Prince Filbert!" chirruped Firetail, recognizing his voice at once. She bounded down the tree to look for him.

"There you are!" called a boy leading a dappled grey horse. "I'm so glad I found you!"

"Prince Filbert!" gasped Firetail as Conker and Mother came to see. "Then the acorn *was* magic after all!"

Prince Filbert shook his head. "It might grow into an oak tree," he said, "but my mother, the queen, is very wise and said the only way to break a witch's curse is for someone to do a kind deed. So it was your kindness, not magic, that saved me, Firetail."

Firetail beamed with delight.

"Then you really were a snowman?" asked Conker.

"I was until your sister rescued me. Now I'd like to repay her kindness and ask you all to live with me in the Faraway Wood."

"We'd love to!" cried Firetail. But then she panicked. "What about the wicked witch?" she said.

The prince laughed. "The king was so angry he banished her from the kingdom!"

"Hooray!" said Firetail then she, Mother and Conker all climbed merrily on to the horse's back.

"Is the Faraway Wood really full of acorns?" enquired Conker as they rode off.

"Overflowing," said the prince. "Now you'll never go short of food."

It was a long journey, but when they got to the palace the king and queen were waiting for them with three silver platters piled high with acorns.

"Tuck in!" cried the prince.

"Try and stop us!" said Conker, and the hungry squirrels ate until their bellies were full.

Finally the prince showed them their new home in a magnificent oak tree right outside his bedroom window.

"It's perfect!" chirruped Firetail, jumping for joy.

From that day on, Firetail and Prince Filbert were the best of friends. Her family lived happily ever after and never went hungry again.

And as for Firetail's magic acorn? Behind the henhouse a new family of squirrels are all living happily in their very own tree...

MAKING
FRIENDS

Linda Chapman

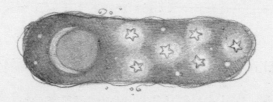

Anna turned the page of her book and snuggled down further into her thick coat. It was cold sitting on the bench in the garden, but she loved being outside even when it was winter. Last year, she and her best friend, Jasmine, had hung up balls of bird food and put nuts out for the squirrels as a Christmas treat. But now Jasmine had moved far away and they couldn't play together any more. Anna felt a wave of loneliness. Christmas wasn't going to be much fun this year.

I wish Santa could bring me a friend. She sighed and looked at her book again. It was about a girl taming a wild pony called Merlin. To stop herself thinking how quiet it was, Anna started reading out loud...

"Josie held out a treat and Merlin came closer, step by step. He watched her warily with deep brown eyes. Josie stayed absolutely still, not wanting to scare him away..."

Anna heard a rustle in the bushes. Was it a bird? Or a squirrel? She couldn't see anything and so she read on...

"Merlin stopped in front of Josie and snorted softly as if he was saying hello..."

Rustle!

Anna looked up and her heart seemed to trip as she caught sight of two dark eyes watching her from the shadows of the bushes. It was a young fox! He had pointed ears, rusty-brown fur and a bushy tail tipped with white.

Anna waited for him to run away, but he didn't. He sat down and looked at her curiously, almost as if he was waiting for her to read on. Remembering what Josie had done in the book, Anna stayed very still, and started to read out loud again.

"Josie let Merlin sniff at her hands and then he gently took the treat. He stood there beside her. Hardly daring to breathe, she slowly touched his long, tangled mane…"

The fox crept closer. Anna didn't feel scared – he didn't look like he was going to bite her. He just looked interested. As he reached the bench, Anna wondered if he would let her stroke him like Merlin had let Josie. If only she had some treats.

"Anna!" Her mum called from the house. "Time to come in for lunch!"

The fox jumped at the sound of her mum's voice and bounded away into the bushes. Disappointment flashed through Anna. She'd wanted him to stay there with her.

She sighed. "Coming!" she called to her mum.

Over lunch, Anna told her mum about the fox.

"Do you think he'll come back?" Anna wanted to know.

Her mum looked doubtful. "I don't think so, honey. Foxes tend to stay away from humans. You were very lucky to have seen him at all."

After lunch, Anna took some ham from the fridge and went outside again. She knew what her mum had said was true, but she couldn't help hoping. She sat on the bench and started to read...

"Josie gently stroked the pony's muddy neck. He stood still, watching her every move. 'Do you want to be my friend?' she murmured."

There was a movement in the bush and the fox reappeared. Still reading, Anna dropped some ham on the floor.

He hesitated then trotted forward and gobbled it up. She fed him more and more until every scrap had gone and all the time she read on. After he had finished the ham, the fox sat down a little way from the bench.

Anna longed to reach out and touch him, but she didn't want to frighten him. In the story she was reading it had taken Josie a long while to tame Merlin so that he would come when he was called and let her stroke him. Maybe she just had to be patient and then the fox would become her friend, too.

Anna read on until it was too cold to stay outside any longer. As she stood up, the fox darted into the bushes. "I'll come back tomorrow," she promised him.

He watched her go.

Anna spent as much time in the garden as she could over the next few days. She named the fox Rusty because of his orangey-brown coat and each day she read to him and fed him more bits of ham. He started to come out from the bushes when she called his name. But on the Saturday before Christmas he didn't come.

"Rusty!" Anna called, puzzled. Where was he?

She heard a whimper coming from the bushes. She hurried over and parted the branches.

"Rusty!" she gasped.

The fox was lying down. He was wounded on his side and his back foot was bleeding.

Anna knelt beside him and he licked her hand. "I'll go and get help," she said and then she raced inside to get her mum.

Ten minutes later, Anna and her mum were on the way to the vet's with Rusty in a cardboard box. Anna had padded it out with towels.

Oh, please be OK, she thought.

It was lunchtime at the surgery and there were no other patients there. Anna's mum had rung on ahead to let them know they were coming and as soon as they arrived, a nurse whisked them into a room where the vet was waiting. He was a

smiley-faced man with a beard. "What have we here then?"

Anna explained about Rusty. Rusty whimpered in the box. The vet said that he would give him an injection to make him sleepy and then he would examine him.

Anna and her mum went back to the waiting room. After a few moments a girl about Anna's age came in through a back door. "Hi, I'm Evie," she said. "Dad told me about the fox you brought in."

Evie had a short ponytail the same colour as Rusty's coat and freckles on her nose.

"I'm Anna," Anna said. "I'm really worried about him."

"Don't worry. My dad'll look after him," said Evie.

"It must be amazing living at a vet's," said Anna, looking around. "I want to be a vet when I'm older."

"Same as me!" said Evie.

The two girls smiled at each other.

"Would you like to come and see the other animals while you wait?" Evie asked. "I'm allowed to help with them."

"Oh, yes, please!" said Anna.

They went through to the recovery room where the sick animals were kept.

Along the walls were lots of different-sized cages. Some were full and others were empty. There was a Golden Retriever dog with a bandaged front leg. He thumped his tail when he saw Evie. "This is Simba. He's broken his front leg. You can stroke him if you want. He's very friendly."

Anna cuddled Simba and then helped
Evie fill up the water bowls for the animals
that were allowed water. After that they
played with a litter of orphaned black
kittens who needed handling so that they
got used to humans. There were four of
them and Evie had called them Sooty,
Sweep, Jet and Ebony.

Finally they gently groomed a long-
haired rabbit called Nibbles who had eaten
some ivy and was feeling very poorly.

"He'll get better," Evie said. "He was much worse when he first came in. You have to be so careful with rabbits. Ivy is poisonous, but so are rhubarb and foxgloves and tomato plants."

At last, Evie's dad came to find them. He took them through to the waiting room. "The news is good," he said. "I've stitched up Rusty's wound and bandaged his paw. He'll need to stay here for a few days so we can keep an eye on him, but then he'll be able to be released back into the wild."

Anna breathed out with relief. Her mum hugged her.

"Can I come and visit him each day?" she asked.

"Oh, yes, please can Anna come?" said Evie. "None of my other friends like looking

after animals," she explained to Anna.

Evie's dad smiled. "Of course Anna can come and visit."

Anna beamed. There was nothing she wanted more in the world!

For the next few days, Anna visited Evie's house every morning. Rusty improved. He had to wear a big white cone round his neck to stop him pulling his bandage off, but Evie's dad was pleased with his progress. He told the girls that although they could talk to him, they mustn't pet him too much – if he got too used to humans he wouldn't be able to return to the wild. Anna was allowed to read to him though and Evie loved listening to the story of Josie and

Merlin, too. Her favourite part was near the end where Josie hurt herself and Merlin let her ride on him so he could carry her back home. That was Anna's favourite bit of the story, too! She loved how the pony and the girl became such good friends.

Just like me and Rusty, she thought. *I wanted a friend and now I've got one.* She smiled as she realized she didn't just have one new friend, she had two!

On Christmas Eve, Evie and her parents came round for mince pies in the early evening. They brought Rusty with them because Evie's dad said it would be a perfect time to set him free.

Anna ran out to meet Evie and her mum

and dad when she saw their car arrive.
Dusk was falling. Evie's dad took Rusty out
of the car in a plastic crate.

"I wish I could keep him," Anna said,
stroking him through the cage bars.

Evie's dad smiled understandingly.
"I know, but Rusty's a wild animal. He
really wouldn't be content living as a pet."

Evie's mum nodded. "He'll be much
happier roaming free."

Anna knew she was right and all she
wanted was for Rusty to be happy.

"And you'll have your hands full with
lots of other animals to love and look after
at the surgery," said Evie's mum. "It's been
great having someone who's as animal-mad
as Evie round the place. I hope you keep
visiting us."

Anna glowed happily. "Oh, I will."

Evie's dad handed Anna and Evie the crate. "Here you go."

The two girls carefully carried Rusty round the side of the house, into the back garden and across the grass to the bench where Anna had first met Rusty. Then Evie stood back while Anna opened the crate door.

The young fox jumped out. He sniffed the air and then bounded towards the bushes. He stopped, turned and looked at Anna. "Bye, Rusty," she whispered. "Come back soon."

Rusty stared at her intently for a moment and then slipped into the shadows.

Anna took a deep breath, feeling both sad and happy at the same time.

Evie squeezed her hand, seeming to

understand. "He will come back," she said.

They stood in silence for a moment and then Evie picked up the crate and glanced at the twinkling stars. "Santa's probably just setting off."

"We'll have to leave carrots for his reindeer," said Anna.

"I wonder what he'll bring us," said Evie.

Anna smiled. Her own Christmas wish had already come true. She had two new friends – Rusty and Evie. No present in the world could be better than that. "Are we still going to meet up tomorrow?"

"Definitely!" said Evie. "I need help giving the animals their Christmas treats and hugs."

"This is going to be the best Christmas ever!" Anna said.

The two girls grinned at each other and then ran back to the house, their boots leaving tracks of footprints side by side on the frosty grass. In the bushes, Rusty watched them go and then trotted happily away.

LITTLE STICK TAIL AND THE MOON DEVIL

Lucy Courtenay

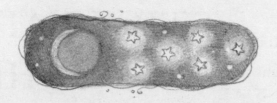

Little Stick Tail lived in the best burrow in the Kalahari. There were insects, beetles and scorpions to eat, water to drink and the sand was perfect for burrowing.

Today, he was going on guard duty for the first time.

"Do you know what to do, Little Stick Tail?" asked Mother Meerkat as the mob burrowed and foraged around them in the late winter sun.

"I do this!" Little Stick Tail puffed out

his chest and stood up tall. "And this!"
He moved his head from side to side
without blinking his eyes. "And this!" He
opened his mouth.

"No!" said Mother Meerkat.

It was too late. Little Stick Tail gave a
loud warning bark.

The other meerkats froze.

"DANGER!" shouted Father Meerkat.

"DANGER!" shouted the other meerkats
in the mob.

Everyone except Little Stick Tail and
Mother Meerkat shot into the burrow.

"Look what you've done, Little Stick
Tail," Mother Meerkat scolded. "The mob
thinks we're under attack!"

Father Meerkat wasn't pleased.

"Go and stand guard at the Furthest

Rock, Little Stick Tail," he ordered crossly
when he came out of the burrow again. "We
must protect our burrow from the Enemy
and watch carefully for eagles and snakes.
And no more false alarms! Three Legs will
take over from you later."

Three Legs had lost a leg to a snake
when he was younger, but was still big and
strong and one of the best guards in the
mob.

Little Stick Tail felt nervous but excited
about standing guard at the Furthest Rock.
He left his mob feeding and digging and
playing, and scampered across the sand
towards his post.

The good thing about the Furthest Rock
was that it gave you a very good view all
around. Little Stick Tail stood as straight

as he could, looking left and looking right, feeling important and not blinking at all.

Guard duty was fun for about five minutes. After ten minutes, it was boring. After fifteen, it was plain dull. Little Stick Tail wanted to run and jump, wrestle with his brothers and eat scorpions. Most of all, he wanted to sit down.

Over at the burrow, the mob was still feeding and playing. There were no eagles. No snakes. No sign of the Enemy.

No one will know, thought Little Stick Tail.

He sat down. He yawned. Even though it was winter, the afternoon sun was hot. If he lay down, he decided, then the sun wouldn't be in his eyes…

He fell asleep.

Little Stick Tail woke up with a start. Just over the top of the Furthest Rock, he heard a strange voice.

"…too many of them now. But I have a plan."

Peeping over the edge of the Furthest Rock, Little Stick Tail saw a gang of strange meerkats gathered beneath him.

The Enemy!

Little Stick Tail was so frightened, he wanted to run back to the burrow. But the Enemy was too close and they'd catch him for sure.

The Enemy's fur was browner than the fur of Little Stick Tail's mob. They looked bigger, too. Little Stick Tail stayed where he was, listening and watching.

"We'll attack their burrow tonight by moonlight," said the biggest meerkat. He had eye patches as black as night and sharp, nasty teeth.

"But we don't go out at night, Alpha!" said a fat one at the back of the group.

"That's why this plan is so brilliant, Muncher," said Alpha. "They won't be expecting us. It's the longest night of the year – we'll have plenty of time. We'll chase

133

them out of that burrow quicker than you can say beetle."

"Beetle," said Muncher. "Just practising, Alpha."

Little Stick Tail stayed lying down until he was sure that the Enemy had gone. They were planning to attack the burrow tonight! He had to warn—

"Little Stick Tail!"

Little Stick Tail shot to his feet. "Three Legs!" he gasped. "The Enemy is planning—"

"Silence!" Three Legs' eyes were fixed angrily on Little Stick Tail. "How dare you lie down on duty? You put the whole mob in danger!"

"But—" Little Stick Tail began.

A dusty-coloured eagle had started

circling overhead. Three Legs barked loudly. Over at the burrow, the meerkat mob rushed for cover.

"You have let us down," Three Legs growled. "We will not forget."

Back at home, Father Meerkat gave Little Stick Tail the scolding of his life.

"But Father—" Little Stick Tail tried to explain about the Enemy's moonlight attack. Father Meerkat wasn't listening.

"You are banned from guard duty," he roared. "You will stay in the burrow and watch the babies until their mothers return from foraging."

Little Stick Tail groaned. "Not the babies! They are so silly!"

"And you are sillier than all the babies put together," said Father Meerkat.

Babysitting was the worst job in the burrow. The babies just squealed and pooed and wriggled around. Little Stick Tail watched them until he thought he was going to die of boredom.

At sunset, the rest of the mob returned to the burrow. Little Stick Tail ran outside at once to take big, fresh gulps of air. The babies were smelly.

The shadows were growing long and the air was already cold. A big winter moon hung in the sky. If the Enemy attacked the burrow, Little Stick Tail and his family would have to survive out here in the bitter chill. Little Stick Tail picked up a passing beetle and put it in his mouth to cheer himself up.

It was a dung beetle.

Dung beetles lived in the burrow with the meerkats and tidied up the meerkat poo. Meerkats enjoyed eating beetles, but there was so much other food around the burrow and dung beetles tasted so awful that they rarely ate them. Just in time, Little Stick Tail spat out the dung beetle and wiped his tongue with his paws.

"What am I going to do?" he said out loud. "The Enemy is going to attack our burrow tonight, but no one is listening to me!"

"I'm listening," said the dung beetle breathlessly. "It's my burrow, too. If it's in danger, I will defend it."

"You're just a beetle," Little Stick Tail scoffed, looking down at the small black creature by his feet. "What can you do?"

"I am one beetle, it is true. But I have ten thousand brothers and sisters."

Ten thousand was a lot. Maybe the dung beetles could help. Little Stick Tail stared thoughtfully at his shadow. It stretched tall and fierce before him in the moonlight. An idea unfolded in his head.

"If ten thousand of you all stood really

close together over there," he said to the
beetle, pointing

at a large stretch

of sand

behind the

burrow, "how much

of that sand would you cover?"

"Loads," said the dung beetle.

"Fetch your brothers and sisters," said
Little Stick Tail. "Ask them to gather as
quickly as they can. I need a tall, spooky
shape on that big patch of sand."

"Why?" asked the dung beetle.

Little Stick Tail tapped his head. "I think
it's time to give the Enemy a little fright,"
he said. And he explained his plan.

Little Stick Tail bravely dashed towards the Furthest Rock. His shadow was fast and black against the moonlit sand. He stood up and waited. The air was freezing. He shivered and stamped his feet to keep warm, and tried not to think about how cold his family would be if they lost their burrow tonight.

At last, he saw the Enemy in the bright winter moonlight, leaping stealthily across the desert.

Little Stick Tail scampered towards them. "Thank goodness you've come!" he gasped.

The Enemy goggled at him.

"You said they wouldn't expect us, Alpha!" said the fat one called Muncher.

Alpha's pointed teeth gleamed in the moonlight. "What are you doing out in the dark, you scrawny rat?"

"I'm escaping from the Moon Devil!" Little Stick Tail said in a scared voice.

"The Moon Devil?" Alpha said in disbelief. "Is this a trick? Where is the rest of your mob?"

"They've run away," Little Stick Tail panted. "I'm the only one left."

Alpha checked the horizon, making sure Little Stick Tail was alone. "Your burrow's empty? How ... interesting." His teeth shone again. "Tell me more about your Moon Devil."

"He comes on the longest night of the year, when there is a full moon," Little Stick Tail explained. "He's invisible, but he always casts a shadow. That's how I know it's him. Come quickly! Help me to fight

him, and then my family can come home again!"

Alpha's eyes gleamed in the moonlight. "Come on, crew," he said. "Let's help the youngster to, er, fight his invisible Moon Devil, shall we?"

The moon dipped behind a cloud as the Enemy started running towards the best burrow in the Kalahari. Little Stick Tail raced ahead of them, crying: "Moon Devil! Moon Devil! Look how many meerkats we are! We're coming to chase you away!"

Some of the Enemy slowed down. Muncher stared around nervously.

"Moon Devils don't exist, you fools!" Alpha hissed, still galloping at full speed. "Take the burrow. Take the—"

The moon scudded out from behind

its cloud. And there, on the big patch
of sand behind the burrow, lay a great
spooky-shaped blackness. It had arms.
It had legs. It had a round black belly.

"Moon Devil, Moon Devil!" cried Little
Stick Tail in glee. "We can see your shadow!"

The Enemy skidded to a halt and spun
round, looking for the monster that could
cast a shadow so big. They saw nothing.

"W-w-where is it?" Muncher gasped through chattering teeth.

"Who knows?" Little Stick Tail said cheerfully. "It's invisible."

The spooky-shaped blackness swayed. There was a strange noise on the wind. A noise that sounded like ten thousand beetles clicking their wings — but only to Little Stick Tail.

"Aargh!" screamed Alpha. "AARGH!"

Sleepy meerkats popped out of the burrow at the commotion as the Enemy ran for their lives, back into the dark and freezing desert, screaming as if something huge and invisible was chasing them in the winter moonlight.

Father Meerkat rubbed his eyes. "Little Stick Tail?" he said. "Did you just chase the

Enemy away all by yourself?"

Behind the burrow, the Moon Devil's shadow broke up into ten thousand beetle-shaped pieces that flowed past Little Stick Tail, past Father Meerkat, back into the best burrow in the Kalahari.

"Not quite by myself, Father," said Little Stick Tail honestly.

"Well," said Father Meerkat with a smile, "I know who will always guard the Furthest Rock from now on."

THE STORY
KITTEN

Holly Webb

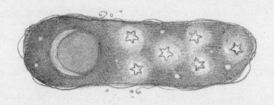

"Tell me again," Lulu begged, clutching at Martha's pyjamas so that her big sister couldn't climb off her bed.

"Again? I've already told you twice tonight, Lulu. It's time to sleep. Mum will be coming up to check on you soon. She'll be cross if we're still chatting."

"No, she won't." Lulu made a pleading face. "She might pretend to be cross, but she'll just stay and listen to the story. You know she will. It's her favourite story, too."

"Oh, all right. But just one more time."

Lulu nodded and curled closer round her sister, and Martha wriggled her feet under Lulu's duvet.

It was a freezing cold night, and their bedroom was chilly. The wind was whistling and the weather forecast had even said that it might snow at the weekend. Not tonight, though, Mum had told them. The sky was too clear.

Martha had looked out at the stars when she'd drawn the curtains. They hung in the sky seeming close enough for her to touch, floating just beyond the branches of the old tree outside the window, caught in a net of its spindly twigs. Martha had thought she could reach out and pick a star, silver and sparkling, and make a wish on it.

"Go on!" Lulu prodded her with one finger and Martha smiled.

"One day…" The story always started the same way. "One day, maybe even quite soon, we'll have a kitten of our very own."

"To keep," Lulu added. That was important.

"Yes, to keep."

"What will it look like?"

"It will be a black kitten. Black as night. But with a little white furry star under its chin and a long black tail, with just a tiny touch of white at the end."

Lulu nodded happily. She knew all this. Martha must have told the story a hundred times by now. But Lulu loved to hear it. Her big sister made it sound so certain. So true. "And we'll call him Sam," Lulu said. Both Lulu and Martha thought Sam was a gorgeous name for a cat. "Will he sleep on my bed?" she asked dreamily.

"Yes, most nights," her sister agreed. "Sometimes he'll sleep on my bed instead. Maybe Mum's bed, too, every so often."

Lulu nodded. That was fair. "And he'll play with us?"

"Yes. We'll have to get him some cat toys. One of those feathery things you wave up and down. And a wind-up mouse to chase."

"But Lucy at school says her cat never

plays with his proper toys. He just steals bits of Lucy's brother's Lego, and chases that all over the house." Lulu frowned. "Maybe we should buy some Lego instead." She was silent for a moment and Martha wondered if she was falling asleep at last.

"Martha, how will we get the kitten?"

Martha frowned. They hadn't thought about that before. Somehow, their beautiful black-and-white story kitten was too special to have come from a pet shop, like any ordinary cat.

"He'll find us," Martha decided. "On a moonlit night, full of stars, just like tonight. We won't know that he's coming. He'll walk straight through the night. And it will be so dark that no one will see him as he goes past. Except for the little white tip of his tail, so it will look like a tiny white star floating by."

"Will Sam be OK, travelling all on his own?" Lulu asked anxiously. "He's only a very little kitten."

"Yes, but he's an adventurer. I should think he's had lots of adventures already." Martha thought for a minute, and smiled. "He's been a witch's kitten, but all those spells made him sneeze, so he had to give that up. And then he was a ship's cat on a pirate ship. But he got sick of nothing but fish to eat. He loves fish, of course. But he likes a change occasionally."

"Smoky bacon crisps," Lulu murmured sleepily. "They're my favourite, too. Did he ever get seasick?"

"Yes, a little bit, just like you. So now he wants to settle down and find a forever home in a house that doesn't sway up and down."

"I just wish it wasn't so dark…" Lulu murmured.

"But dark's good for a black kitten," Martha reminded her. "And he can see perfectly in the dark, too."

Lulu suddenly sat up in bed. "What colour are Sam's eyes?" she asked excitedly. "I've forgotten."

Martha knew that she hadn't really. The kitten's eyes were one of Lulu's favourite parts. "They're green," she reminded her sister. "But not a bright green. A soft blue-green, like the sea. Maybe because he did some of his growing up on a pirate ship," she added. "His eyes are like the sea around the treasure islands."

"Perhaps he really is coming tonight..." Lulu suggested, her eyes shining. She pulled the duvet up to her chin and stared hopefully at Martha. "Where is he now?"

"I said a moonlit night, Lulu. That's all. A night *like* tonight. Not actually, really tonight."

"But it could be," Lulu said stubbornly. "It could be tonight. Couldn't it?"

"I suppose so," Martha sighed. She snuggled her cold toes further in, underneath the backs of Lulu's knees, and closed her eyes. She loved this story, too,

but she had told Lulu about the kitten so many times now. She just wished it was all true. Or that they could have any everyday cat. She wouldn't mind if it wasn't their little black story kitten. She would love a tabby cat, or a ginger. A white cat even. She wouldn't care if the kitten that turned up was purple, to be honest, as long as it was theirs.

Mum had said that they could have a cat one day, when they were a bit older. But she never said when. Martha sighed and Lulu prodded her again.

"Where is he, Martha? Where's Sam now?"

"Just walking towards school. He's come all the way across the fields and through the bluebell wood."

"Through the woods! What about the foxes? And the badgers?" Lulu squeaked. She had been for walks in the woods and they had seen the badger holes. They looked big.

"He slipped past them all. Some of the time he went through the trees, jumping from branch to branch and tree to tree, like a squirrel. And even if a fox did try to chase him, his claws are needle-sharp and he fights like a pirate. He probably has a spell or two still hidden in those whiskers, as well. There might be a really confused fox back in those woods, a green fox that keeps wanting to say 'Ribbit' and doesn't know why."

"I suppose so," Lulu agreed. "But I still don't like to think about it. All those big,

dark, shadowy trees, with things lurking behind them, maybe. Urrrghh."

"He'll be walking past the school now. He might even take a shortcut through the playground and see your classroom. And then he'll slip through the railings and out on to the street. He'll be coming the same way that we walk home from school."

"Oh! He'll go past all my favourite places!" Lulu said excitedly. "Is he going to go past the swings?"

"Yes. He might go down the big slide. Or maybe the scramble net. That would remind him of the pirate ship, when he used to climb the rigging and sit in the crow's nest with the look-out. Then he'll be almost at our road." Martha sighed silently. She could picture it. The little black kitten, stalking

through the shadows,
stopping here and
there to pounce
on a fallen leaf, or
sniff at an interesting
smell floating out from
under a hedge.

"Our road! Do you think he'll see Freddy and Coco?"

The girls stopped every morning on their way to school to say hello to the cats who lived close by. Coco was a fat white Persian with a plumy tail and Freddy was ginger, with emerald-green eyes. There was a pond in his back garden and his owner, Mrs Dane, was always telling Lulu and Martha about the strange places Freddy had found to leave the frogs he caught. Once she had woken up

to find Freddy next to her on the bed and a small, very worried frog sitting on her pillow.

"I hope Freddy and Coco like Sam," Lulu murmured. "Is he nearly at our house?"

"Yes." Martha nodded. "He's slipped down the alleyway, past the wheelie bins. The gate's locked, so he wriggled under the hedge."

"He's in the garden!" Lulu gasped. "But we don't have a cat flap, how's he going to get in?"

Martha eyed her worriedly. "It's only a story, Lulu, remember."

"I don't care! Tell me!"

"Ummm. He'll climb the tree." Martha nodded towards the window. It was still windy and the branches were tap-tapping against the glass. It was a spooky sort of noise, but the girls were used to it.

"I can hear him!" Lulu stared wide-eyed at the window. "Mewing! Didn't you hear, Martha?"

"That's the wind. Sam's just a story, Lulu. One day we'll have our own cat, but this one's just a story kitten."

"It *was* him," Lulu said stubbornly. She pushed back the duvet, and climbed out of bed. "You'll see."

Martha sighed, and followed her little sister to the window. Lulu was hesitating, her fingers on the curtains, as though she didn't quite dare to pull them back. She wanted to believe so much – she didn't want to see just the darkness, and the tree...

Martha put her arm round Lulu's shoulders and drew the curtains open. "You see," she said. "I'm really sorry, Lu."

The wind mewed, louder and louder, and Martha shivered.

But Lulu had frozen next to her. "Look," she whispered. "It's him. Just like you said. Oh, Martha! He's come."

Martha looked out of the window, her heart thumping so hard she felt dizzy.

Balanced on the spindly branch was a small black kitten, with a white-tipped tail, mewing loudly and rather crossly now, as if to tell them to hurry up and let him in.

Blinking, Martha turned the key and pushed the window open. The kitten stepped daintily down the branch and jumped on to the sill. His black fur was ruffled with the cold, but his sea-green eyes were shining. He rubbed his head against Lulu's cheek and peered mischievously up at Martha.

"Just like you said," Lulu whispered again, as she gently wrapped her arms round the little black kitten and cuddled him. "You came all that way, Sam. Martha said you would. Oh, Martha, you're so clever."

"I wished," Martha murmured. "I wished, and he came."

THE MOON
THIEVES

Elizabeth Baguley

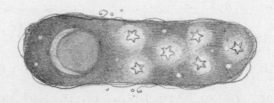

Inside the villa, everything was ready for a feast. The roast swans glistened, the sweetmeats lay in honeyed piles. Precious gifts were hidden in corners, waiting.

Waiting, too, was Lucius. He stood in the villa courtyard, holding a candle and whispering a prayer to the top of the mountain where the gods lived: "Selene, Selene, bring us the Moon. Selene, Selene, bring it soon."

It was the night of the great Winter

Feast, held in honour of the Moon Goddess, Selene. Like all Romans, Lucius and his family were waiting for the full Moon to climb into the sky, pulled by Selene on her silvery horse, Argentea. Then, and only then, would the feast begin.

"Where are you, Moon?" Lucius asked.

"Don't worry," said his mother, finding him outside. "The Moon will rise soon enough. It always does."

"But what if it doesn't, Mother?" asked Lucius. "We won't be able to have the feast and all the food and presents."

"Be patient, Lucius — and while we're waiting, I'll tell you the story of a Winter Feast when the Moon almost didn't rise. It happened long, long ago and it happened like this…"

On the mountain towering above the Earth where Selene and the other gods live, something terrible had happened. Selene's horse, Argentea, was limping. "Astra, do you know how this happened?" Selene asked her daughter.

"It was just a game, Mother," said Astra, hanging her head. "I was playing at acrobats with Argentea."

"And you startled her?"

"Yes, Mother," said Astra. She remembered suddenly springing on to the horse's back. Argentea had wheeled round in surprise, giving a cry of pain as she twisted a foreleg. Astra had been thrown, landing on the frosty ground with a thump.

"It's the mortals' Winter Feast tonight," said Selene. "It can't begin until the Moon rises. You know that we have no other animal who can pull the Moon along the Sky Road."

"But you'll be able to make Argentea better, won't you?" asked Astra in alarm.

"Of course," replied Selene, "but even a goddess's healing hands won't be able to make her well in time for tonight's Moonrise."

Astra bit her lip while she thought for a moment. Then she had an idea.

"We could harness a unicorn instead, couldn't we, Mother?" she asked.

"Oh, Astra," said Selene. "I think you've done enough damage for one night. Unicorns are wild – even wilder than you are. They're almost impossible to catch and we'd never persuade one to pull the Moon. They simply don't like to work. I'm afraid that we can't take the Moon over the Sky Road tonight. Now, I must go and look after Argentea. And you must try to keep out of trouble."

Astra watched her mother hurry into the stable. Looking down the mountain she could see the faint glimmer of the mortals' candles lit in honour of her mother and, straining her ears, she heard their whispered prayers for the Moon to rise.

If she didn't make up for what she had done, they would think it was her Mother's fault and that simply wasn't fair. And they'd have to wait for a whole year before the next Winter Feast, poor things. Astra herself wasn't good at waiting for anything. She knew just how they'd feel. Well, it was up to her to put it right.

Astra crouched on a high rock, her tunic torn and her knees scraped. In her hand lay the fragile flower that she had scrambled so high to pick. She was in the night-dark Winter Fields, a high-sided gully on

the mountainside, always deep with snow. The place was ringing with cold, from the frozen lake to the frost-whitened trees. Snowflakes flew through misshapen crags on a bitter wind. Her mother said it was dangerous here. But this was where the wild unicorns lived.

Astra knew where to look for them. She'd often watched them, climbing the stony outcrops in search of the snow-flowers, rare as comets, that they loved above all other food. They ran faster than water, their hooves leaving hardly a trace in the snow.

Now she just needed to spot a unicorn, though the land seemed empty and barren, whiteness upon whiteness.

Then something moved from behind

the waterfall, turning from a pale shadow into a strong, living beast. A silken white animal with a milky, twisted horn walked towards the rock where Astra perched – the perfect animal to pull the Moon.

If only she could tame him, little by little, slowly teaching him to work, like a horse.

But there was no time for that.

As the creature walked beneath her, Astra flung herself into the whirling snow, dropping like a stone to land stomach down on the unicorn's broad back.

"Caught you!" she muttered. But for the second time that evening, she was thrown from a startled animal's back and found herself lying crumpled on the ground. She hadn't caught the unicorn at all. He was cantering away from her with a triumphant toss of the head.

Quickly she picked up the flower, which had fallen on to the snow, and held it out. Catching its tempting scent, the unicorn turned to look. Astra dared to stare back.

"Come on, Wild One," she said. The unicorn turned an ear at the sound of her voice. For a moment his sea-deep gaze locked on to her own. Then without warning he dashed past her, snatched the flower and ate it, kicking his heels as though he was laughing at her.

Astra smiled. "I see," she said. "You'd rather play than work, is that it? Maybe we could play together! We could..." She tried to think of an exciting make-believe game that the animal might like. "We could pretend to be Moon thieves."

The unicorn listened excitedly with bright eyes. He made a rumpling noise through his nostrils and his hooves danced like wind-blown candle flames.

"You're a bright one!" said Astra, realizing that the animal understood. "So I'll call you Clarus! Now, Clarus, are

you ready to steal the Moon?"

She vaulted on to Clarus's back and urged him towards home. This time, he did not throw her off.

And so the game began.

Playing Moon thieves was easy for Astra, whose imagination was as wild as her hair. She pretended that the Moon was guarded by a hundred-headed hound that had fallen asleep.

"We need to hitch the Moon to you before the dog wakes," she said, "or he'll bite us for certain." Immediately Clarus wanted to get away from the imaginary dog and so he reversed towards the ice dome where the Moon was kept. Astra had no time to find Argentea's harness so she'd snatched up a wiry strand of frozen ivy instead. Once she'd roped Clarus to the Moon, Astra pretended that she'd woken the imaginary dog and it was chasing them. In an instant Clarus galloped away along the Sky Road with Astra clinging on.

The glass Sky Road rose to the top of the sky before looping downwards to the other side of the mountain. Clarus's hooves skimmed across its slippery surface, pulling the spinning, bouncing globe.

Astra fizzed with excitement as they rode. The Moon was rising and the mortals' Winter Feast had surely begun. How grateful they'd be.

"Faster!" she urged Clarus, completely lost in her game. "Now soldiers are

coming to catch us."

Clarus put in a spurt of speed. Neck stretched forward, he was determined to pull the stolen globe so fast that they would never be caught.

Astra could do nothing but hold on. The Moon began to wobble, then rock. Its bumping and buffeting jolted her out of her fantasy. They were hurtling towards the top of the sky with uncontrollable speed.

"Slow down!" shouted Astra. "We might lose the Moon if we're not careful!"

Clarus's speed was making it lurch from side to side like a storm-tossed ship. The faster they went, the more the Moon swayed. A terrible tearing noise told her that the ivy harness was fraying under the strain.

And then, to her horror, it snapped.

Over her shoulder, Astra watched the Moon rumbling and rolling dangerously back down the road towards the mountainside where the gods lived. They had to catch it. She wheeled Clarus round to give chase.

"You are a flying unicorn," pretended Astra, but although Clarus almost did fly, he wasn't fast enough to catch up with the

runaway Moon.

The great globe careered onwards. It was sure to break as it crashed into the mountainside. The Moon would be gone forever. Astra closed her eyes and groaned.

Then the rolling stopped. With a sound like the strings of a harp all being plucked at once, the Moon smashed into its ice dome at the bottom of the Sky Road and was still at last. Immediately behind it, Astra and Clarus skidded to a halt amongst the heap of broken ice.

A little while later, Selene, who had rushed to see what had made the noise, was soothing the shocked unicorn to sleep.

"At least you're both safe," she said, turning to her daughter. "Astra, you shouldn't have done this. You risked both your lives."

"I know I've been bad, Mother," Astra admitted, "but I wanted to make the Moon rise so that the mortals wouldn't miss their Winter Feast. So that they'd still believe in your goodness."

"Oh, my little wild child," said Selene, her voice softened with pride.

"And I'm so sorry about the ice dome."

Selene sighed and hugged her daughter. "I may have an idea about that," she said. "Something that will keep you out of trouble."

And with a wave of her hand each shattered piece of ice dome began to spit and spark with bluish light.

"Let's call them stars," said Selene, picking up some of the glittering fragments. "They will be hung in the night sky to give light, Moon or no Moon. We'll need someone fearless to hang them there, someone riding a courageous beast. Maybe a unicorn..."

"And so it was," said Lucius's mother. "Astra and Clarus became the greatest of friends. Their favourite game was to gallop together into the spinning night to play at sky artists. They made star pictures of bears and scorpions, goats and fish – and if you look carefully, you'll see a picture of a unicorn, too."

Lucius looked to where his mother was pointing, but the starry unicorn was outshone by a great circle of light rising above the Earth.

"It's the Moon!" shouted Lucius. "Let the Winter Feast begin!"

OBI'S
UMBRELLA

Caroline Pitcher

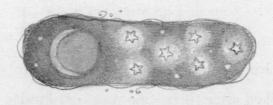

Little Obi Orangutan woke and gazed out of his enclosure.

A cold white moon sat in the sky. Obi wanted to climb up to it, but all around was a hard, criss-cross pattern of wire. Everything was pale in the moonlight.

As Obi watched, soft white flakes began to drift downwards and he wondered if the moon was made of feathers.

His mother puckered her lips and touched his forehead in a kiss. "Did the moonlight wake you?" she asked. "It's very bright tonight. Soon it will be dawn and Kira will come to see us."

Kira was their keeper, the human who looked after them. She was very kind.

Obi shivered and his mother said, "Snuggle up and listen – I'll tell you a story to help you go back to sleep."

He wrapped his long arms round her and snuggled close.

"Once upon a time," she began, "there was an orangutan who lived in a great rainforest. Her name was Oralie. That means 'golden'. Oralie's hair was rich gold. She lived high up in the forest canopy."

"What's a canopy?"

"The canopy is the treetops. It's a roof of leaves. It makes everything look cool and

green, dreamy as a forest pool."

"Was Oralie on her own?" asked Obi.

"Yes. When her mother had another baby, Oralie was six and old enough to fend for herself. So off she went."

Obi stroked his mum's silky fringe. In the moonlight it shone crimson and bronze. He said, "But wasn't Oralie lonely?"

"No. Orangutans don't live in noisy packs like gibbons, or crash around in herds like elephants, or flap about in flocks like hornbills. Orangutans are clever and independent."

"You sound very proud of being one, Mum," said Obi.

"I am," she said. "So Oralie lived in the leafy canopy under the bright blue sky. One day she heard someone swinging towards her through the trees. A voice called, "Whoo-ah? Whoo-ah?" And that was when she met an orangutan called Uba."

Obi's mum turned her face away shyly.

"And?" pestered Obi.

"Uba was handsome, majestic and strong. He had the biggest cheek-pads Oralie had ever seen. Uba became the father of Oralie's baby."

Obi twiddled his mum's whorled ear. It looked like a little golden flower. He asked, "So what was this baby like?"

"He was beautiful! He had a dear face with a domed forehead, and bright round eyes to melt your heart. His hair was russet red." His mother sighed deeply, and when she turned her face to look down at Obi, he saw tenderness and love.

"What happened to Uba?" he asked.

"Oh, he went off again on his travels. Orangutan mums look after their babies much better by themselves."

"And were they happy, the mum and the baby in the great big rainforest?"

"Yes. Oralie and her baby travelled through the wide spaces, grasping hold of creepers and branches. The rainbow birds fluttered away, but they soon settled back when they saw that the orangutans meant them no harm. Those days were wonderful. Oralie leaped from tree to tree with her baby clinging tight to her, chattering with joy."

"I'd love to be that baby," whispered Obi. "I'd love to go flying through the forest, living life without a care in the world."

Obi's mum tidied the hair on the top of his head and said, "Maybe you can get back to sleep now?"

"No," he cried. "I want to hear the end of the story. Please go on."

His mum said dreamily, "Every day, when Oralie travelled through the treetops with her baby, she pictured the special orangutan map in her head. She could remember where the best trees were and when they had their fruit. And every night, she built a nest."

"A nest? Like a bird makes?"

"Yes, but Oralie's nest was much, much bigger. She climbed to the top of a tree and built a nest out of branches and leaves. She slept there with her tiny baby, under the glittering stars, and they were as comfortable as orangutans can ever be. And each morning the sunlight woke them."

"Mum, that sounds like paradise," chirruped Obi.

"But the paradise didn't last," said his mother sadly.

"What happened?"

"One morning, they heard a harsh sawing sound. It made them cover their ears. When it finally stopped, they smiled at each other in relief. But then an alarm call echoed through the trees. Oralie knew it was Uba, warning them, before he fled away to safety."

"Why was he warning them?"

"He was saying, 'Look Out! Danger!' They saw a tree topple as it was cut, screaming and crashing to the ground. It terrified all the birds and insects and animals that lived in it, tore the creepers and flattened the flowers on the forest floor. One by one, the trees fell."

"That's awful," whispered Obi. He began to suck his thumb. "Why did they fall?"

"Because the humans cut them down. Humans have to live on the ground. They're not so good at climbing trees as we are."

"But why do they take them?"

Obi's mum closed her eyes. "I don't know. They must want the trees for something, or they wouldn't steal them from the rainforest. Soon, it wasn't green and shady any more. It was open to the sky. There were no hiding places, no fruit to eat and no places to make nests."

"So what did the orangutans do?"

Obi's mum's eyes darkened. "Oralie told her baby to hold on tighter than ever. She ran along the ground, hoping they could escape to a safe place."

"Did she find one?"

"No. Instead, she and her baby became tangled in a net. Some humans threw it over them. However much they struggled and cried, they just couldn't get free. Oralie and her poor baby bumped around in this net until they were exhausted. Then they heard chickens squawking and saw a cage. The humans shooed the chickens out and put the orangutans in instead. It smelled of birds."

Obi saw sadness fill his mother's eyes and reached up to pat it away.

"It must have been horrible," he whispered.

"It was," she murmured, "and it was so frightening."

"Did they give Oralie and the baby anything to eat?" asked Obi.

"No. Some children came and stood on the other side of the cage. They were babies, like you, Obi. The children smiled at the orangutans and a female baby in a pink dress blew kisses to them and the other children joined in."

"They liked the orangutans!" cried Obi.

"They certainly did," said his mother, "and they wanted their parents to be kind to them. So at last, the humans shrugged their shoulders and nodded their heads to their children. A noisy van arrived with gentle humans inside, who gave the captors some shiny coins. They counted them and laughed. The gentle humans carried the orangutans out from the chicken coop to the van and drove along a bumpy road. Then they loaded them on to a plane for a long, long journey. They were shut in the dark for ages, and all the while there was a dull roaring noise. The end of that journey was … here at the zoo, with Keeper Kira!"

Obi stared at his mother. He cried, "So you're Oralie, the orangutan who had the baby!" He looked at his mother's silky hair, crimson gold in the morning light, her neat little nostrils and wide smiley mouth in her coconut-shell face. "And I was that little baby."

"Yes! But when all this happened, you were too little to remember."

The key turned in the lock. The door opened and there stood Kira.

"Hello, my lovelies!" she said. "How are

you, this cold morning?"

"Whoo-ah!" they grunted.

"Today is very special," said Kira. "It's Christmas Day. It's a day of gifts and I've got two gifts for you. The first one is a promise. I promise that you are going on an aeroplane, very soon..."

"An aeroplane?" Obi shivered.

"That's fine, Obi," Oralie soothed him, whispering low so that only he could hear. "Remember I said you travelled on a plane when you were tiny? You slept in my arms most of the way."

Kira went on. "And soon you'll be carried off the plane to a safe part of the forest where there are no loggers, no noisy saws and no humans lopping down your precious trees. Oralie and Obi, you are going home!"

The two orangutans hugged each other with joy.

"I'll just get the other gift…" Kira went off. She returned a moment later, carrying something wrapped up in red sparkly paper. "The second gift is for you, Obi, and it looks like I've brought it just in time." She took Obi's hand and led him outside into the swirling moon feathers. One of them landed on Obi's head with a cold splodge. Obi caught more feathers in his hand and put them to his mouth. They made an icy drink.

"It's called snow," said Kira.

She helped Obi to unwrap the sparkly gift. Inside, there was a wooden stick.

Obi stared at the gift. What could it be? Warily, he stretched out his finger and stroked the fabric attached to it. It was cool and smooth. Then he touched a little button lightly – and nothing happened. He pressed it again, and out opened a canopy shaped like a big flower, patterned in red and blue.

Kira showed him how to hold it over his head, to shelter him from the snowflakes. Oralie came outside to join Obi under his new canopy.

"It's called an umbrella," Kira said, and smiled to see the orangutans enjoying their new Christmas present.

A few weeks later, Obi chose another umbrella. A very different one.

He was sitting high in a tree in the rainforest with his mum, eating the sweetest, juiciest golden fruit, when he felt a pitter-patter-splash! These weren't snowflakes, white and feathery like pieces of the moon. They were raindrops, clear and shiny like diamonds, and they splodged cold on Obi's shoulders.

So Obi chose his very own umbrella.

It didn't have a wooden handle, or a button that opened a red and blue canopy, but it was even better. It was a very different umbrella, one that he made all by himself – the biggest, finest, glossiest emerald leaf he could find, with a long, strong stalk. The raindrops just bounced off it, and Obi held his umbrella high to shelter himself and his mum, back in their rainforest home.

Have you read…?

A Collection of Adorable Animal Stories

MOONLIGHT
Magic

Illustrated by
Alison Edgson

WINTER
Magic

A Spellbinding Collection of Christmas Animal Tales

THE
SNOW
BEAR

FROM BEST-SELLING AUTHOR
HOLLY WEBB

The
Reindeer
Girl

From best-selling author
Holly Webb